Dear Bobby,

As you navigate the journey from child, through adolescence, and on into adulthood, we can

Under the Rose Apple Tree

THICH NHAT HANH

think of no wiser and kinder

guide than *Thich Nhat Hanh.*

May the wisdom in this book be a blessing for your life.

Love,

Mom + Dad

Parallax Press
Berkeley, California

2010

Parallax Press
P.O. Box 7355
Berkeley, California 94707
www.Parallax.org

Parallax Press is the publishing division of Unified Buddhist Church, Inc.

This book is a compilation of Dharma talks given by Thich Nhat Hanh to children during the annual summer retreats at Plum Village, a practice center in the south of France.

Author photo by Don Farber.
Cover illustration by Philippe Ames.
Text and cover design by Crowfoot Design.

Library of Congress Cataloging-in-Publication Data
Nhât Hanh, Thích.
    Under the rose apple tree / by Thich Nhat Hanh.
       p. cm.
    Summary: Presents teachings, stories, and practices that are
       meant to help the reader "touch the Buddha inside."
    ISBN 1-888375-04-3
       1. Spiritual life—Buddhism—Juvenile literature.
       [1. Spiritual life—Buddhism. 2. Buddhism.] I. Title.

BQ5405 .N5 2002
294.3'444'083—dc21

                             2002007871

1 2 3 4 5 6 7 8 9 10 / 06 05 04 03 02

CONTENTS

Listen, listen,
This wonderful sound brings me back
to my true home.

INTRODUCTION BY THICH NHAT HANH

When I was nine, I saw an image of the Buddha sitting peacefully on the grass on the cover of a magazine. Right away I knew that I wanted to be peaceful and happy like that too. Two years later five of us boys were sitting together talking about what we wanted to be when we grew up. We explored many different fields; one boy said he wanted to be a doctor, another said an engineer, and so on. But after a while, we found that nothing really appealed to us.

Then my brother Nho said, "I want to become a monk." This was a novel idea, but I knew I also wanted to become a monk. In part it was because of the picture on the magazine.

Then one boy said, "Why don't we all become monks?" It was children's talk, but in fact all five of us did become monks. One boy became a Catholic monk, and the other four of us became Buddhist monks. And to this day, three of us are still monks.

The seed of becoming a monk was planted deeply in me after that discussion. I really wanted to become a monk, but I knew for my parents it would be difficult to accept because the life of a monk is a very modest one, and they wanted their children to enjoy the good things in life. I knew that I had to carefully prepare them.

I kept a diary and from time to time I wrote about my aspiration to become a monk. One day I asked my mother to read my diary to my father so that they would get accustomed to the idea. It was too hard for me to do it directly by myself. In that way, going slowly, step by step, I won the approval of my parents and was allowed to go to the temple. I became a novice at the age of sixteen.

Thich Nhat Hanh, also known affectionately as Thầy (teacher), is a Zen Buddhist monk who has taught four generations of monks and nuns in Vietnam and in the West, as well as thousands of lay practitioners.

You Are a Buddha-to-Be

The name "Buddha" comes from the word "bud," like a flower bud. "Bud" means to awaken, to understand, and to know. Buddha is one who is awake, who is aware of everything that happens in the present moment. The depth of his or her understanding and love is very great. Anybody can become a Buddha. We are all Buddhas-to-be. We are all future Buddhas, capable of having deep understanding and a great ability to love and relieve the suffering of others.

Friends of the Buddha usually greet each other by joining their hands to make a lotus. The lotus is a beautiful flower that looks like a magnolia. We put our palms together while breathing in and silently saying, "A lotus for you." Then we bow, breathe out, and silently say, "A Buddha-to-be." We offer this gesture as a gift.

The Buddha said that there are many other Buddhas everywhere who are teaching, trying to bring love and compassion into everyday life. The Buddha said, "All of you are Buddhas-to-be." He was right, because in each of us there are seeds of understanding, love, and compassion. When we cultivate love and understanding, we water those seeds, and they will blossom and bear fruit. If we practice according to the teachings of the Buddha, we will become Buddhas.

Each of us is a Buddha-to-be. That is why we want to live in a way that allows the Buddha in us to blossom. When we know how to breathe, how to walk, how to smile, how to treat people, plants, animals, and minerals, we become real Buddhas.

TOUCHING THE BUDDHA INSIDE

In Buddhist texts, called "sutras," the most important message is that everyone has the capacity to be a Buddha — the capacity to love, understand, and be enlightened. This is the most important message from all the sutras.

The practice I would like to show you is called "Recollection of the Buddha," and it is taught in every school of Buddhism. You touch the Buddha inside you and all the qualities of the Buddha, and you know that the Buddha is absolutely real — not an idea, not a notion, but a reality. Our task, our life, our practice is to nourish the Buddha in us and in the people we love.

You may like to spend three or four minutes on this practice, either alone or together with a few friends. Sit down quietly, breathe in and out for a few minutes to calm yourself, and then ask, "Little Buddha, are you there?" Ask the question very deeply and quietly. "My little Buddha, are you there?" In the beginning, you might not hear an answer. There is always an answer, but if you are not calm enough, you won't hear it. "Anyone there? Little Buddha, are you there?" And then you will hear the voice of your little Buddha answering, "Yes, my dear, of course. I am always here for you."

Hearing this, you smile. "I know, little Buddha, you are my calm. I know you are always there, and I need you to help me be calm. Often, I am not as calm as I'd like to be. I scream, I act as if I do not have the Buddha in me. But because I know you are there, I know I am capable of being calm. Thank you, little Buddha, I need you to be there." And the little Buddha says, "Of course I'll be here for you all the time. Just come and visit me whenever you need to." That is the practice of touching the Buddha inside. It's a very important practice for all of us.

I love to sit close to children because of their freshness. Every time I hold the hand of a child and practice walking meditation, I always benefit from his or her freshness. I might be able to offer the child my stability, but I always benefit from his or her freshness. If you lose your peace and joy, remember that you have been fresh many times in the past. And if you touch the Buddha, the freshness in you will continue to grow.

You can say to the Buddha inside of you, "Dear little Buddha, you are my freshness. Thank you for being there."

"Dear little Buddha, you are my tenderness." Tenderness is what all of us need.

"Dear little Buddha, you are my mindfulness." And that is true, because a Buddha is someone who is made of the energy of mindfulness. To be mindful means to be aware of what is happening, and that is only possible when you are really there, one hundred percent there. Whenever you act mindfully — drinking a glass of milk, walking, or breathing mindfully — you are touching Buddhahood, you are touching your Buddha nature.

"Dear Buddha, you are my understanding." Understanding is so crucial. If you don't understand someone, you cannot love him or her. The Buddha is the power of understanding. When you are mindful and aware of everything that is going on inside you and around you, you understand things and people very easily. So you can say, "Little Buddha, you are my understanding. I need you very much because I know that understanding is the foundation of love."

"Dear little Buddha, you are my love. You are the capacity of loving." You, too, have the capacity to love. If you touch that capacity every day, your love will grow, your capacity to love will grow, and you will be on your way to fully realizing the Buddha within yourself.

Every time you visit the Buddha, the Buddha in you benefits. The Buddha in you will have more space and air to breathe. During the day, you may have suffered, you may have been very angry, and that deprives the Buddha inside you of fresh air to breathe. Your little Buddha may be suffocating. But every time you practice touching the Buddha, you bring in a lot of space and air, and the Buddha within you has a chance to grow. It's very important.

If you practice touching these qualities of the Buddha in you, you touch the real Buddha, not the Buddha made of plaster, copper, or even emeralds. Buddha is not a god. Buddha is not someone outside of us, up in the sky or on a mountaintop. The Buddha is alive and living in us.

"Dear Buddha, it is very comforting to know that you are there. Little Buddha, I need you very much." And the little Buddha in you will say, "Dear one, I also need you very much. Please come and visit more often."

INVITING THE BELL

In the old days when there were no telephones, people who lived far from each other were not able to talk. When the telephone was invented, it was like a miracle. You are used to the telephone, so you don't see how wonderful it is, but it's really a miraculous invention. Every time we use the telephone and hear the voice of a loved one living far away, we become very happy. The bell is a kind of telephone because listening to the sound of the bell is like listening to the voice of someone dear on the telephone.

The sound of the bell could be described as the voice of the Buddha, calling us home, reminding us to be more at peace with ourselves and with the world. We pay loving attention to that voice. Listening to the bell can be very wonderful, and it can bring us a lot of peace and joy. It can bring us back to our true home.

When we are away from our true home for a long time, we long to return to it. In our true home, we feel at peace. We feel we don't have to run anywhere and that we are free of problems. We can relax and be ourselves. You are already what you want to be. It's wonderful to be the way you already are. You don't need to be something else, someone else.

Look at the apple tree. It's wonderful for the apple tree to be the apple tree. It does not have to become something else. How wonderful that I am myself. How wonderful that you are yourself. There is no need to try to be something else or someone else. We only need to let ourselves be what we already are, and enjoy ourselves just as we are. That feeling, that realization, is our true home. Each of us has a true home inside.

Our true home always calls to us, day and night, in a very clear voice. It keeps sending us waves of love and concern, but they don't reach us because we are so busy. So when we hear the bell, we remember that it is helping us to go back to our true home, and we let go of everything — talking, thinking, playing, singing, being with friends, or even meditating! We give it all up and go back to our true home.

When you listen to the sound of the bell, the Buddha of the bell, don't talk or think or do anything, because you are listening to the voice of a person you love and respect a lot. Just stand quietly and listen with all your heart. If there are three sounds, listen and breathe deeply during the entire period with concentration. Breathing in, you feel fine; breathing out, you feel happy. Feeling happy is very important. What is the use of breathing and practicing if you don't feel fine, if you don't feel happier? The deepest desire in each of us is the desire to be happy and to bring happiness to the people and living beings around us.

You might like to invite the bell yourself. Here is how to do it. First, hold the bell up high, leaving the bell cushion on the floor and using your open hand as a cushion. Your open hand holding the bell looks very beautiful, like a chrysanthemum or a lotus flower with five petals open. Our hand is the lotus and the bell is the precious jewel in the lotus. We can look at it and say, "Oh, the jewel that is in the lotus," or in Sanskrit, *om mani padme hum.*

Put the bell on your lotus flower hand, raise it to your forehead, look at it, and smile. Then breathe in and out three times while you silently recite the following *gatha* (poem):

Body, speech, and mind in perfect oneness,
I send my heart along with the sound of this bell.
May the hearers awaken from forgetfulness
And transcend the path of anxiety and sorrow.

It's OK if, as you ring the bell, you happen to forget this gatha, but do your best to remember it.

We breathe in and recite the first line:

Body, speech, and mind in perfect oneness.

This means you have concentration.

Then with your out-breath:

I send my heart along with the sound of this bell.

This means you send your love to the world.

Say on your in-breath:

May the hearers awaken from forgetfulness.

Forgetfulness is the opposite of mindfulness, and the sound of the bell helps us to be mindful. Hearing the voice of the Buddha, the sound of the bell, we come back to the present moment.

On your out-breath, say:

And transcend the path of anxiety and sorrow.

After you have practiced breathing in and out like this while reciting the gatha, you will feel much better; your mind and body are now united, you are concentrated, and you have the beautiful wish that everyone who hears this bell feels no sorrow, anger, or anxiety, and that they enjoy breathing and smiling.

Now that you are feeling much better, you are ready to invite the bell to sound. When inviting the bell, we always give a wake-up sound first to prepare the bell and to prepare everyone for the full sound of the bell so that they are not surprised by it. It is not a full sound. We touch the bell inviter to the bell; this is called "waking up the bell." Everyone stops thinking and talking and gets ready to receive the sound of the bell, because the sound of the bell is considered to be the awakening voice of love and compassion. Everyone prepares himself or herself for the call of the Buddha.

Between the waking-up sound of the bell and its real sound is the space of one breath. So you practice breathing in while waiting for the real sound, and then invite the bell so that the real sound comes. We say "Invite the bell to sound," not "Hit the bell," because we want to be kind and not do violence to the bell.

Those who are listening to the sound of the bell silently recite the following gatha:

Listen, listen,
This wonderful sound brings me back
    to my true home.

Listen, listen means we listen with all our concentration while we breathe in, and with our out-breath, we smile and say, *This wonderful sound brings me back to my true home.* The sound of the bell is the voice of the Buddha in you, calling you back to your true home, the home of peace, tolerance, and love.

PRACTICING MINDFULNESS

There is no happiness or peace without mindfulness. Mindfulness is remembering to come back to the present moment. Everything we are looking for is right here in the present moment. If we allow ourselves to be in the present moment, we have the capacity to touch wonderful things. But if we do not allow ourselves to be in the present moment, we will continue to struggle.

Mindfulness helps us to live more happily and to see the beauty of things more deeply. When you look at the full moon with mindfulness, it is much more beautiful. When you hug someone with mindfulness, that person will be more real and sweet.

Breathing in, she's alive.
Now, she's in my arms.
Breathing out, I'm so happy.

Without mindfulness, you are not really alive. Being mindful makes everything you do brighter, more beautiful. When you look at a flower with mindfulness, the flower reveals its beauty to you deeply. To practice mindfulness is to be happy and to enjoy what the moment brings you, including all the wonderful things inside of you — your eyes, your heart, your lungs — and all the wonderful things outside — sunshine, people, birds, trees. Through mindfulness, you will find that you have even more reasons to be happy than you thought.

Mindfulness also helps to heal pain. When pain comes in touch with mindfulness, the pain begins to slowly dissolve. If you have pain but don't know it, that pain will stay with you for a long time. When you are aware of your pain and you embrace it with the arms of your mindfulness, then that pain begins to transform.

When you are in pain, you can use your mindfulness to hold your pain tenderly, just as a mother who takes her crying baby into her arms to quiet him or her. If you embrace your pain in this way, it will transform. A crying baby should not be left unattended; neither should your pain.

In the early morning, the flowers are closed, but if the sun shines, tiny particles of sunshine penetrate into the flowers, and you soon see a transformation. Each flower opens and shows itself to the sun. Our suffering is like that; if we expose it to the light of mindfulness, it will change.

Stopping

Learning how to live deeply in the here and now begins with the practice of stopping. There is a well-known Zen story about a man on a galloping horse. Someone watching him ride by shouts to him, "Where are you going?" The rider turns and yells, "I don't know, ask the horse."

This story may be funny, but it is also true. We do not know exactly where we are going or why we are rushing. A galloping horse is pushing us and deciding everything for us. And we follow. That horse is called "habit energy." You may have received this energy from your parents or your ancestors. Your words and actions are dictated by this energy and you do not have sovereignty over yourself; it is not you but the horse that is pushing you forward. It is the habit energy that makes you do and say things in spite of yourself. This causes harm to you and others.

For example, even though we know that if we say something mean to someone, we will create suffering for ourselves and for those around us, we still say it. Later we may regret it and say, "I couldn't help it. The urge was stronger than me." Then we sincerely promise ourselves that the next time we will not say mean things. But when the situation arises again, we do exactly the same thing, saying and doing things that are hurtful not only to others but to ourselves, as well. This kind of energy is habit energy.

Our task then is to become aware of this habit energy and to not let it push us around anymore. We can smile at it and say, "Hello there, my habit energy, I know you are there." So, the first way to take care of yourself is to learn how to stop and look inside. This is a very wonderful practice.

When we become agitated, when someone is angry or screaming, when we are very sad or depressed, what can we do to smile again and be alive? If we learn the art of stopping, we can calm things down within and around us. The purpose of stopping is to become calm, clear-sighted, and solid. If we are not calm, clear-sighted, and solid, we cannot confront our problems.

Stopping does not mean sitting still. Even if you sit still in one place, your mind can be drawn into the past, the future, or to your projects, and that is not stopping. Inside of us there is a video that plays all the time, nonstop; you think of this or that, you see one image and then another. It never stops. So even if you don't say anything aloud, there is no silence within. Silence inside helps us enjoy what is here in the present moment. It allows us to look at the sunset and really enjoy it.

So stopping is going back to the here and now and touching the wonders of life that are available now. Without stopping, your mind is not in union with your body — your body may be sitting in one place, but your mind is somewhere else. Stopping brings your body and mind together, back to the here and now.

An important part of our practice is looking deeply in order to see. We often suffer because we don't look carefully and we have misconceptions. It is like someone walking on a path at night who sees a snake and, frightened, runs into the house, screaming, "A snake!" Everyone runs out, and when a light is shone on the "snake," it shows that the snake is only a rope on the path. So in order to take care of ourselves, to calm things down in and around us, we practice stopping and looking deeply.

By stopping — sitting quietly, just breathing in and out, being silent within — you become more solid, more concentrated, and more intelligent. Your mind is clear, and you react well because you are solid and strong. Now you can look deeply at what is happening inside and around you.

SITTING UNDER THE ROSE APPLE TREE

Sitting meditation is one of the ways to return to the here and now. Meditation is a wonderful way to stop. If we know how to practice sitting meditation, we will become clear, strong, and solid. Then it will not be easy for anyone to provoke us or to make us lose our composure. So you sit like a mountain. No wind can blow the mountain over. If you cannot sit for a half-hour, sit for only three minutes. If you can sit like a mountain for three minutes, that is already very good.

When you sit, make sure that you are not sitting for anyone else; sit for yourself. Why do I sit? Because I like it. Don't say, "I sit because I want to obtain Buddhahood." If someone asks you why you sit, say, "I sit because I like it." That is the best answer, I think. You enjoy sitting because you become a flower, a mountain, still water, and empty space. When you become all these wonderful things, you become truly yourself, living deeply in the here and now.

Here is a story about Siddhartha, the Buddha, when he was a boy.

When Siddhartha was nine years old, he and his schoolmates were allowed to attend the ceremony of the first plowing of the fields. Each year King Suddhodana presided over this ceremony. Gotami, Siddhartha's mother, dressed Siddhartha in his finest clothes for the occasion.

The ceremony was held in one of the most fertile fields in the kingdom. The priests began by reciting from the holy scriptures. Then the King, with the help of two military officers, plowed the first row of the field as a crowd cheered them on. The plowing season had begun! Following the King's lead, the farmers began to plow their own fields.

Siddhartha stood at the edge of one of the fields and watched a farmer hitch a water buffalo to his plow. Steadying the plow with one hand, the farmer whipped the water buffalo with his other hand. The buffalo strained hard under the weight of the heavy plow. The sun blazed down on the farmer, his body glistening with sweat. The plow divided the rich earth into two neat furrows.

Siddhartha noticed that as the earth was turned by the plow, worms and other small creatures were being cut in half and left to die in the hot sun. Birds flying overhead spotted them and came to feast. A hawk swooped down, grasped one of the birds in its talons, and carried it off.

Standing beneath the burning sun watching these events, Siddhartha, too, became drenched in sweat. He ran to the shade of a rose apple tree to reflect on all he had seen. He sat down and crossed his legs. He closed his eyes. He sat for a long time, still and straight, thinking about what he had seen in the field. As he sat there, family members began coming to the field with refreshments to celebrate the occasion of the first plowing. There was singing and dancing. But even after the festivities began, Siddhartha continued to sit quietly.

Siddhartha was still absorbed by what he had seen in the field, when the King and Queen passed by. They were surprised to see Siddhartha sitting with such deep concentration. His mother was moved to tears when she saw how beautiful Siddhartha looked. When she approached Siddhartha, the boy looked up and said, "Mother, reciting the scriptures does nothing to help the worms and the birds."

Later, when the Buddha had been practicing for a long time, he thought back to when he was nine years old and sat in meditation for the first time beneath the cool shade of a rose apple tree on the day of the year's first plowing, and recalled how refreshing and peaceful those moments had been!

If sitting were unpleasant and required a lot of effort, I would not sit at all. I sit only because it makes me happy. I would not sit if it made me suffer. To sit in meditation means to be there with one hundred percent of yourself. If at first you are there with only eighty percent, that is good enough. You will get better and better all the time. Maybe yesterday it was eighty percent, but today it may be eighty-one percent. The more present you are, the happier and more solid you become. Sitting is only for your happiness and stability, not for someone else's.

When we sit and meditate, we stop and let our minds become calm and clear. It is like mud settling in water. If you put mud into a glass of water and let it sit, the mud will slowly settle to the bottom and the water will become clear. If you stir or swirl the mud around, it will not have a chance to settle. When the mud is calm, the water is clear. The same is true of your mind.

When you sit, feel free to sit in any position — the lotus, half-lotus, chrysanthemum, or half-chrysanthemum positions. The lotus position is the cross-legged position. The chrysanthemum position is whatever position you like.

Choose the position that is most comfortable for you. The lotus position is considered by many to be the most beautiful and stable position. If I sit in this position, then my body is very stable; even if you push me, I will not fall over. When our bodies are stable, our minds are stable too, because body and mind influence each other.

Can meditation affect our unhappiness? Yes, it can. Through meditation, happiness becomes more real and important, and unhappiness begins to diminish. Through meditation our garbage is transformed into compost, and it will soon become flowers again. Through meditation we learn to practice being happy and making other people happy. This is how we take care of our unhappiness.

PLANTING SEEDS OF HAPPINESS

You have both seeds of happiness and unhappiness in you, planted by your parents, ancestors, or your friends. When seeds of happiness manifest themselves, you feel quite happy. But when seeds of sorrow, anger, and hatred manifest, you feel very unhappy. The quality of our life depends on the quality of the seeds in our consciousness.

When you practice breathing, smiling, and looking at the beautiful things around you, you are planting seeds of beauty and happiness. That is why we practice things like breathing in and seeing ourselves as a flower, breathing out and feeling fresh; breathing in and seeing ourselves as a mountain, breathing out and feeling solid like a mountain. This practice helps us plant seeds of solidity and freshness in ourselves. Every time we walk with calm and ease, or smile and release, we are planting seeds that will strengthen our happiness. With each happy step, we plant a happy seed.

Happiness cannot be separated from suffering. We know happiness because we know suffering. If we have not experienced hunger, we cannot fully realize how happy we can be if we have something to eat. If we have not lived the life of a homeless person, we will not appreciate fully the fact that we have a home to live in. That is why happiness cannot be separated from suffering. It means that if you have suffered, you can be happy. If you do not know anything about suffering, you cannot be a happy person.

BREATHING MEDITATION

"When I breathe in, I know that I am breathing in." The "I know" is very important. Your breath is the link between your body and your mind. It's so nice when you are in touch with that link; then you are in touch with everything in yourself, body and mind. And right away, you are master of yourself in any situation. You are not carried away by anybody or anything, including your thoughts. Your mind is fully with your body and your whole being. When you start to know that you are breathing in or that you are breathing out, you start to know what you are doing — whether you are sitting, standing, or walking. So knowing is very important.

Don't think that practicing Buddhism is very difficult. It's not difficult; it's easy. Can you breathe in and out and know that you are breathing in and out? Breathing in and breathing out — that is mindfulness. Practice being mindful with your breath first, and then you will be mindful with your body and with your mind; you will be mindful about everything that happens around you.

Breathing consciously, mindfully, is a very good practice. In our daily life, if we don't know how to breathe mindfully, how to stop thinking, we cannot get in touch with the wonderful things in life like the sunshine, rivers, clouds, our family, and our friends. So breathing is very good.

Mindful breathing is easy to practice, and very enjoyable. Here is a gatha, a poem, that you can say to yourself as you sit for a few minutes and breathe:

Breathing in, I know I am breathing in.
Breathing out, I know I am breathing out.
In/Out.
Breathing in, I see myself as a flower.
Breathing out, I feel fresh.
Flower/Fresh.
Breathing in, I see myself as a mountain.
Breathing out, I feel solid.
Mountain/Solid.

Breathing in, I see myself as still water.
Breathing out, I reflect things as they are.
Water/Reflecting.
Breathing in, I see myself as space.
Breathing out, I feel free.
Space/Free.

First, practice "In/Out" three times. "Breathing in, I know I am breathing in. Breathing out, I know I am breathing out. Then move to the exercise called "Flower/Fresh."It means, "Breathing in, I see myself as a flower. Breathing out, I feel fresh."

The third line is "Mountain/Solid." "Breathing in, I see myself as a mountain." The cross-legged position is a very stable and solid position. If you manage to sit cross-legged, breathing silently and smiling, you will be as solid as a mountain; you will not be blown away by any emotions, thoughts, or winds from any direction. So, "Breathing in, I see myself as a mountain. Breathing out, I feel solid."

The fourth exercise is "Water/Reflecting." Looking at the clear and still lake water, you can see the sky and clouds reflected in the water as clearly as when you look up at the sky and clouds themselves. Have you had this experience? "Breathing in, I see myself as still water. Breathing out, I reflect things as they are." It means, I don't distort things. Don't say, "I *feel* like still water." Say, "Breathing in, I see myself *as* still water." We are ourselves the water. We are ourselves the mountain. We are ourselves the flower. I reflect exactly the blue sky that I see. I don't distort things, because I am clear, I am solid, and I am calm.

Still water is very calm. When you are calm, you reflect reality well. When you are not calm and still, you perceive things incorrectly and distort them. It is like seeing a piece of rope and thinking it's a snake. Because you are not peaceful or calm enough, you don't reflect reality as it is. Have you looked in one of those funny mirrors that distorts images? Looking in those mirrors, you can hardly recognize yourself; your face is long and your eyes are big. Have you had that experience? It is not how you really look.

The last line in the exercise is "Space/Free." "Breathing in, I see myself as space." With space, you feel so at ease. If people give you enough space or freedom, you will be happier. When you breathe in, you see yourself as infinite space — space in which everything moves freely — and you can breathe. Without that space, you cannot breathe or smile.

When you are empty, you do not keep anything within yourself — no hatred, anger, despair, or craving. As empty space, you feel wonderful. When you breathe out, say, "I feel free." "Breathing in, I see myself as space. Breathing out, I feel free." Try it.

The images of flower, mountain, water, and space will help you to have better concentration and to feel refreshed, stable, calm, and free.

Another breathing exercise you can practice during your sitting meditation is this: "In/Out, Deep/Slow, Calm/Ease, Smile/Release, Present Moment/Wonderful Moment."

Breathing in, I know that I am breathing in.
Breathing out, I know that I am breathing out.
As my in-breath grows deep,
My out-breath grows slow.
Breathing in makes me calm,
Breathing out brings me ease.
With the in-breath, I smile,
With the out-breath, I release.
Dwelling in the present moment,
I know this is a wonderful moment.

"Breathing in, I know that I am breathing in. Breathing out, I know that I am breathing out." That is the first verse. Then, "As my in-breath grows deep, my out-breath grows slow." You recognize the quality of your breath now. You don't want to make it long or deep, you just recognize it as being deeper and slower now. After doing that a few times, you move to "Calm/Ease."

"Breathing in makes me calm. Breathing out brings me ease." Ease is like space, it is the feeling of being light and free. You cannot be happy unless you are light and free. Ease means do not take anything too seriously; nothing is more important than your peace.

"With the in-breath, I smile." Why smile? You smile because you don't take anything too seriously. You know the benefits of smiling. When you smile, all the muscles on your face relax. You see what is important and what is not important. "With the out-breath, I release." You are able to smile at the unimportant things and let them go. This is release. Release is the source of happiness.

"Dwelling in the present moment, I know this is a wonderful moment." You need only to allow yourself to be in the present moment and you will be able to touch these conditions of happiness.

The practice is easy. Peace and happiness are there to some extent, along with pain and suffering. But remember, like watching television, you are free to select from the channels made available to you. You can choose peace and happiness.

YOU HAVE NEVER BEEN BORN

When you look at the sheet of paper you are reading from, you may think that it did not exist before it was made at the paper mill. But there is a cloud floating in this sheet of paper. If there were no cloud, there would be no rain, and therefore no tree could grow to give us this piece of paper. Even if you are not a poet, you can see a cloud floating in this piece of paper, and if you remove the cloud from the paper, the paper will collapse. Looking deeply into this sheet of paper, touching it deeply, you can also touch the cloud.

Shall we ask whether this paper existed before it was born? Has it come from nothing? No, something never comes from nothing. The sheet of paper "inter-is" with the sunshine, with the rain, with the Earth, with the paper factory, with the workers in the factory, with the food that the workers eat every day. So the nature of the paper is interbeing. If you touch the paper, you touch everything in the cosmos. Before its birth in the factory, the paper was the sunshine, it was a tree.

You may also think that when you were born, you suddenly became something from nothing; from no one, you suddenly became someone. But actually, the moment of your birth in the hospital or at home was just a moment of continuation, because you had already existed in your mother for nine months. That means your birth date on your birth certificate is not correct; you have to push it back nine months earlier.

So now perhaps you believe that you have the truth, that the moment of your conception is the moment when you began to exist. But we should continue to look deeply. Before the moment of conception, were you a nothing, a no one? Before that, half of you was in your father, and the other half was in your mother, in another form. That is why even the moment of conception is a moment of continuation.

Imagine the ocean with its multitude of waves. The waves are all different; some are big, some are small, some are more beautiful than others. You can describe waves in many ways, but when you touch a wave, you are always touching something else — water.

Visualize yourself as a wave on the surface of the ocean. Watch as you are being created — you rise to the surface, you stay a little while, and then you return to the ocean. You know that at some point you are going to end, but if you know how to touch the ground of your being — water — all your fears will vanish. You will see that as a wave, you share the life of the water with every other wave. This is the nature of our interbeing. When we live only the life of a wave and are not able to live the life of water, we suffer quite a lot.

So the reality is that you have never been born — if you define birth as becoming something from nothing, becoming someone from no one. Every moment is a moment of continuation. You continue life under new forms, that's all.

When a cloud is about to become rain, it is not scared, because although it knows that being a cloud floating in the sky is wonderful, to be the rain falling down on the fields and oceans is also wonderful. That is why the moment a cloud becomes rain is not a moment of death, but a moment of continuation.

There are people who think that they can reduce things into nothingness. They can eliminate people, they can kill someone like John F. Kennedy, Martin Luther King, Jr., or Mahatma Gandhi, with the hope that they will disappear forever. But the fact is that when you kill someone, that person becomes stronger than before. Even this sheet of paper cannot be reduced to nothing. You have seen what happens when you put a match to a piece of paper. You cannot reduce the piece of paper to nothing. It continues on as heat, ashes, and smoke.

BUDDHA AND MARA

When we talk about what a Buddha is, we also have to talk about what a Buddha isn't. The opposite of the Buddha is Mara. If the Buddha is enlightenment, then there has to be something that isn't enlightenment. Mara is the absence of enlightenment. If the Buddha is understanding, then Mara is misunderstanding, and if the Buddha is loving kindness, then Mara is hatred or anger, and so on. If we don't understand Mara, we can't understand the Buddha.

Just as a rose is made of non-rose elements, the Buddha is made of non-Buddha elements, and among those elements is Mara. If the garbage does not exist, then the rose doesn't exist either. This insight is so important, it completely transformed my understanding of the Buddha.

When you look at a rose, you may see the rose as immaculate and very beautiful. And the opposite of a rose is garbage, which is not beautiful and does not smell very good. But if you look deeply at the rose, you will see that the garbage is in there, before the rose, after the rose, and also right now. How is this possible?

Gardeners don't throw away garbage. They know that with care, in just a few months, the garbage will become compost which can then be used to grow lettuce, tomatoes, and flowers. Gardeners are capable of seeing flowers or cucumbers in the garbage. Yet, they also know that all flowers become garbage. That is the meaning of impermanence — all the flowers have to become garbage. Although garbage stinks and is unpleasant, if you know how to take care of it, you can transform it back into flowers. That's what the Buddha described as the nondualistic way of looking at things. If you look at things in this way, you will understand that the garbage is capable of becoming a flower, and the flower is capable of becoming garbage.

Every time you practice mindfulness — when you live mindfully — you are in Buddha. When you live in forgetfulness, you are in Mara. But don't think that the Buddha and Mara are enemies that spend all day fighting with each other. No. They are friends. Here is a story that I wrote.

One day, the Buddha was staying in a cave, where it was cool. Ananda, the Buddha's attendant, was practicing walking meditation near the cave, trying to intercept the many people that always came to visit the Buddha so that the Buddha wouldn't have to receive guests all day long. That day, as Ananda was practicing, he saw someone approaching. As the person drew near, Ananda recognized Mara.

Mara had tempted the Buddha the night before the Buddha became enlightened. Mara had told the Buddha that he could become a man of great power — a politician, a king, a president, a foreign minister, or a successful businessman with money and beautiful women — if he gave up his mindfulness practice. Mara had tried very hard to convince the Buddha, but it had not worked.

Although Ananda felt very uncomfortable at the sight of Mara, Mara had already seen him, so he could not hide. They greeted each other.

Mara said, "I want to see the Buddha."

When the head of a corporation doesn't want to see someone, she asks her secretary to say, "I'm sorry, she is in a conference now." Even though Ananda wanted to say something like that, he knew it would be lying and he wanted to practice the fourth precept of no-lying. So he decided to speak what was in his heart to Mara.

"Mara, why should the Buddha see you? What is the purpose? Don't you remember how you were defeated by the Buddha under the Bodhi tree? How can you bear to see him again? Have you no shame? Why should he see you? You are his enemy."

Mara was not discouraged by the Venerable Ananda's words. He just smiled as he listened to the young man. When Ananda had finished, Mara laughed and asked, "Did your teacher really say that he has enemies?"

This made Ananda very uncomfortable. It didn't seem right for him to say that the Buddha had enemies, but he had said it! The Buddha had never said that he had enemies. If you are not concentrating very deeply or mindfully, you may say things that are contrary to what you know and practice. Ananda was confused. He went into the cave to announce Mara, hoping that his teacher would say, "Tell him I am not at home!" or, "Tell him I'm in a conference!"

To Ananda's surprise, the Buddha smiled and said, "Mara! Wonderful! Ask him to come in!"

Ananda was baffled by this response from the Buddha. But he did as the Buddha said and invited Mara in. And you know what the Buddha did? He hugged Mara! Ananda could not understand this.

Then the Buddha invited Mara to sit in the best spot in the cave, and, turning to his beloved disciple, said, "Ananda, would you like to go and make some herb tea for us?"

As you may have guessed, Ananda was not very happy about this. Making tea for the Buddha was one thing — he could do that a thousand times a day — but making tea for Mara was not something he wanted to do. But since the Buddha had asked him to do it, he could not refuse.

Buddha looked at Mara lovingly. "Dear friend," he said, "how have you been? Is everything okay?"

Mara replied, "No, things are not okay at all, they are very bad. I'm very tired of being Mara. I want to be someone else, someone like you. Wherever you go you are welcome, and people bow before you. You have many monks and nuns with lovely faces following you, and you are given offerings of bananas, oranges, and kiwis.

"Everywhere I go," Mara continued, "I have to wear the persona of a Mara — I have to speak in a convincing manner and keep an army of wicked little Maras. Every time I breathe out, I have to blow smoke from my nose! But I don't mind these things so much even; what bothers me more is that my disciples, the little Maras, have begun to talk about transformation and healing. When they talk about liberation and Buddhahood, I cannot bear it. That is why I have come to ask you if we can exchange roles. You can be a Mara, and I'll be a Buddha."

When the Venerable Ananda heard this, it frightened him so much, he thought his heart would stop. What if the Buddha decided to exchange roles? Then Ananda would have to be Mara's attendant! Ananda hoped the Buddha would refuse.

The Buddha calmly looked at Mara and smiled. "Do you think it is easy to be Buddha?" he asked. "People are always misunderstanding me and putting words into my mouth. They build temples with statues of me made from copper, plaster, gold, or even emerald. Large crowds of people offer me bananas, oranges, sweets, and other things. Sometimes I get carried in a procession, sitting like a drunk person on heaps of flowers. I don't like being this kind of a Buddha. So many harmful things have been done in my name. So you can see that being a Buddha is also very difficult. Being a teacher and helping people practice is not an easy job. In fact, I don't think you'd enjoy being a Buddha very much. It is better if we both continue doing what we are doing and try to make the best of it."

If you had been there with Ananda, and if you had been very mindful, you might have felt that Buddha and Mara were friends. They met each other like day and night, like flower and garbage coming together. This is a very deep teaching of the Buddha.

Now you have an idea of what kind of relationship exists between Buddha and Mara. Buddha is like a flower, very fresh and beautiful. Mara is like garbage — smelly, covered with flies, and unpleasant to touch. Mara is not at all pleasant, but if you know how to help transform Mara, Mara will become Buddha. And if you don't know how to take care of the Buddha, Buddha will become Mara.

Looking at things in this way, we know that the non-rose elements, including the garbage, have come together in order to make the rose possible. So the Buddha is something like a rose. But if you look deeply into the Buddha, you see Mara; Buddha is made of Mara elements. And when you understand this Buddhist teaching, you see the emptiness of everything, because nothing has its own absolute existence. A rose is made of non-rose elements, so it has no separate existence; that is why it is called empty. A rose is empty of a separate self, because it is always made of non-rose elements.

Interbeing includes everything — not only Buddha and Mara, roses and garbage — but also suffering and happiness, good and evil. Take suffering, for instance. Suffering is made of happiness, and happiness is made of suffering. Good is made of evil, and evil is made of good. Right is made of left, and left is made of right. *This* needs *that* to be. Removing *this, that* will disappear. The Buddha said, "This is, because that is." This is a very special teaching of Buddhism.

So the practice of Buddhist meditation begins with the acceptance of the rose and the garbage in us. When we see the rose in us, we are happy, but we are aware that if we don't take good care of it, it will quickly become a piece of garbage. Therefore, we learn how to take care of it so that it will stay with us longer. When it begins to deteriorate into garbage, we are not afraid, because we know how to transform the garbage into the rose again. So when you witness a feeling of distress, if you look deeply into that feeling, you will see a tiny seed of happiness and liberation in it. That is how transformation takes place.

Like Leaves on a Banana Tree

One day I was contemplating a young banana tree. I took the banana tree as the subject of my mindfulness, my concentration, my meditation. This was a very young banana tree with only three leaves. First, there was a big sister leaf, then a second sister leaf. The third and youngest leaf was still curled up inside.

When I looked at these banana leaves deeply, I saw that the big sister had her own life to live. She unfurled herself, enjoying the sunshine and the rain, and she was a very beautiful leaf. She gave the impression that she only cared about herself. But if you looked deeply, you could see something entirely different. Because while she enjoyed her life as the first leaf, she was helping the second and third leaves, and even a fourth leaf that was not yet visible but had already formed inside the trunk of the banana tree. She was doing the work of nourishing the whole banana tree.

Each minute of her life, this first leaf practiced breathing and smiling. Through the roots of the banana tree, she received the nutrients which she transformed into nourishment for herself. She then sent this nourishment back to the tree and all her younger sisters and sisters-to-be. She lived her own life and yet her life had meaning; she was helping to nourish and raise future generations.

The second leaf was doing exactly the same thing. She lived her life as a leaf fully, but she also did the work of teaching, nourishing, and bringing up her younger sisters. But if you did not look deeply, you would not see that the first and second leaves were doing the same thing at the same time. The third leaf, though the youngest, would in no time at all be unfurling herself, too. She would soon become a beautiful leaf and take care of her younger sisters.

The same is true for you. By living your life beautifully, you can nourish your sisters, your brothers, and future generations. It is not through sacrificing your life that you help future generations; it is by living your life fully and happily.

When young people say, "I have my own life to live," or "This body is mine, and I can do whatever I like with it," this is not reality. It is a misconception. We are not separate from each other. Your body is not just yours, it belongs to your ancestors, grandparents, and your parents. It also belongs to your children and grandchildren who are not yet born, but who are already present in your body.

You and your parents are one reality. If your parents suffer, you suffer. If you suffer, your parents suffer. If we look deeply and see clearly, we will see that there is just one reality. When you look in that way, you will see clearly that happiness is collective, and you will not go looking for your own individual happiness anymore. You will see that we have to work together and understand one another.

WHEN THINGS
GET DIFFICULT

Families sometimes experience a lot of pain and anguish. When one person in a family has pain, he may spread that pain to other people. For example, even though the love of a father for his child is always there, sometimes he may not be able to show it. In fact, he may seem to show the opposite. But love is present in his heart, and he needs to find a way to express it.

If no one in a family is capable of listening, there will be tension and it will be hard to breathe. No communication will be possible. Happiness is not possible when people don't listen to each other. If, as soon as you open your mouth, the other person says, "I don't want to hear you. I already know what you're going to say. You only want to hurt me," then sharing becomes frustrating, and we turn away from each other.

To be truly happy, we need to be understood. Sometimes you might feel like you are not loved or understood. Because of this, you suffer. To love someone, we must first try to understand him or her. Therefore, we practice sitting and listening; this is the practice of love. Please remember this. Do not give in to prejudices and assumptions; do not think that you already understand the other person.

If we believe the person we love has caused our suffering, we suffer a lot. If another person causes our suffering, we do not suffer as much. But when it is the person we love, we cannot bear it. We suffer one hundred times more. We want to lock ourselves in our room and cry. We don't want to see or talk to him or her. Even if he or she tries to approach us, we are still angry. We don't want to be touched. We say, "Leave me alone!" This is normal.

When this happens, it is better not to respond with words. Just practice "stopping." That's what I do. I return to my breath and say to myself, "Breathing in, I know I am irritated. Breathing out, irritation is still there." I continue to breathe like this for three or four breaths, and there is a change.

Then we have to go to the person we love who just hurt us deeply. We go to him or her with full awareness, mindfulness, and concentration, and say: "I am suffering, please help." This is quite difficult to do, but if we train ourselves, we can do it. We go to him or her, breathe in and out deeply, become ourselves one hundred percent, and say that we suffer and need his or her help. We may not want to do it, because we don't feel that we need his or her help. We may want to be independent and say, "I don't need you," because we feel deeply hurt. That's why we cannot ask for help; our pride is hurt. But it is very important to train ourselves to ask anyway.

We may have to train for some time to be able to practice this. Our natural tendency is to say and to show that we can survive without him or her. This comes from our intention to punish. We want to punish the other person because he or she has dared to make us suffer. But, if we look deeply at the situation, we see that this is unwise. We feel sure that our suffering is caused by him or her, but maybe our perception is wrong. When we love each other, we need each other, especially when we suffer.

ANGER AS AN UNINVITED GUEST

I recently had the opportunity to speak with an American Vietnam veteran, who told me many interesting stories about his transformation, his peace, his joy, and his capacity to be with people, because he has had a hard time being with people. He had been a soldier during the Vietnam War and he had the nature of a soldier. He was ready to face any challenge. If anyone wanted to fight him, he was ready to respond.

But he said that after a few months of mindfulness practice, he had changed. One day he was walking down the street and someone who was very angry approached him and wanted to have a fight with him. Suddenly our friend felt that he did not have the desire to fight anymore.

The man was very angry and wanted to hit him to make him suffer, but our friend did not want to fight. That was a very strange and new idea to him. He practiced breathing in and out and told the man, "If you want to hit me, it's OK. But I will not retaliate because I don't want to fight. I won't fight."

When you strike a stone, although the stone does not strike back, you will get hurt. And that is what he wanted to convey to that person. His face and his voice were calm and did not express anger, so the other person responded in kind. He stopped his aggression and went away.

Our friend congratulated himself. It was his first real victory over his anger. I would like you to practice like he did if you are challenged by another girl or boy to fight. There is a better way to respond to anger than fighting.

When anger rises, breathe in and out and say, "Hello my anger. Breathing in, I know that anger is present. Breathing out, I try to smile." When you are angry, hundreds of muscles are tense, and you look like a bomb, ready to explode. But if you know how to breathe in and out and smile, even if it is not a smile of joy, even if it is only mouth-yoga smiling, it brings about relaxation.

This is a very important practice, because when we are angry we have a tendency to be interested only in the person whom we think is the source of our anger. But actually the source of our anger is here in our minds, in the way that we are thinking.

Anger is like a seed. You have the seed of anger planted inside you already, by your parents, a friend, or even yourself, and you have been watering it every day. Every time you get angry, that seed grows stronger.

The part inside of us where this anger lives is called our "store consciousness." Store consciousness is like the basement of a house. In that basement, there are many seeds; you can think of them as guests. From time to time, you invite these guests into the living room. For example, when you want to sing, you invite the seeds of songs to come up as guests from your store consciousness. Sometimes, however, uninvited guests come into your living room, guests who just push open the door and enter on their own.

It is very unpleasant to have your anger come up as an uninvited guest. It can be so unpleasant that you may want to repress your anger. You might tell your angry thoughts, "Stay down there, don't come up here, I don't want you." Consciously or unconsciously, you decide that you don't want your angry thoughts coming into the living room and making you unhappy, so you push them down. They might stay suppressed for some time, but they will try to come up when you are not being mindful. They can be very tricky too and come back in disguise so that you won't recognize them.

When you are angry, it affects the landscape of your mind. If you don't know how to handle your anger, it will grow and invade the whole landscape. Once you are angry, you are no longer interested in the many beautiful, refreshing things in the world; you are only interested in focusing on the person who has made you unhappy. The more you continue to think about the person who has made you angry, the angrier you get — you are, in effect, fueling your anger. This is what we do every day.

We can learn to be aware of the presence of an uninvited guest like anger, and we can invite something else in to take care of our anger: mindfulness. "Breathing in, I know I am irritated. Breathing out, I know irritation is still in my living room." By saying this, we are being mindful of the anger in us.

When a mother goes to her crying baby and takes the baby in her arms, she does not try to stop the baby from crying by covering his mouth or hitting him. She lets the baby cry and, at the same time, embraces him with love, tenderness, and calm. Little by little, the baby becomes calmer and less agitated until finally, he stops crying. She does not force the baby to stop crying, she envelops him with tenderness and calm. This is how we should treat our anger, too.

Mindfulness is not something with which to fight or repress our anger. Mindfulness helps us take good care of our anger. Practice like this: "Breathing in, I know that I am angry. Breathing out, I know anger is still in me." When you say this, you are still angry, but you are safe because mindfulness is taking care of your anger.

So use mindfulness as a light to shine upon all corners of your consciousness so that it can transform your anger. When something painful comes up, we usually want to bottle it up, and that creates bad circulation in our consciousness. And when there is bad circulation in our consciousness, we are not healthy. So every time pain wants to come up into your living room, you know what to do — don't send it away or suppress it. Stay mindful, and you will be protected. Let it come up. Say, "Good morning, my fear," or "Good morning, my anger. You are my old friend." Practice breathing in and out. If you do this and are mindful, you will be safe. Don't be afraid.

In the same way that a mother takes care of her crying baby, we invite mindfulness to come up and take care of anger when it is born in our mind consciousness. When you say, "Breathing in, I know I am angry. Breathing out, I know I am angry," mindfulness holds your anger in its arms like a mother holding her baby with love and tenderness.

FINDING A CALM PLACE

When we stop running and touch the present moment deeply, we calm down and make our situation easier to deal with. We are like a tree deeply rooted in the ground. Sometimes when the wind blows hard, small branches and leaves at the top violently sway back and forth — the tree looks very vulnerable, fragile. We become so angry or depressed that we think we are going to die. But if we look down, we can see the solid branches and roots and know that the tree is much more solid than we might have thought.

When you are swayed by your emotions, look down and see how solidly protected you are by the roots, the soil, and the trunk of your tree. Embracing the trunk, you will feel that it is very solid. Every time you feel yourself moving back and forth by the force of an emotion, go down to trunk level. The trunk is a little bit below the navel, so go to your abdomen and follow its movement. Breathe according to the gatha, "In/Out," and think of nothing. Focus all your attention on your breathing and the movement of your abdomen — "In/Out, In/Out, Deep/Slow."

You can practice this while sitting on the school bus, walking on the beach, lying down or sitting, when you're alone or with friends. But don't put off practicing until you have a problem. We should practice when we are feeling fine, too, so when we have a problem the practice will be easier. If you practice when you are OK, it will be easier to practice when there is a problem. You will naturally go back to your breathing. Inhale and your abdomen rises naturally, exhale deeply and your abdomen falls. Stay in the moment as you breathe.

LOVING KINDNESS

So many human beings are destroyed by war, political oppression, social injustice, and hunger. If we are not motivated by the mind of love, if we cannot touch the source of compassion in ourselves, we will not have the time or energy to help rescue living beings who are dying every day. To protect life, prevent war, and serve living beings, we need to cultivate the energy of loving kindness every day.

Practice loving kindness everywhere, with everyone and everything. We all need to be protected and rescued. The more we move in the direction of practicing loving kindness, the more we receive the joy, peace, and love of the cosmos. Our feeling of loneliness will disappear.

If we feel lonely, if we feel that there is no love available to us from our society, our family, from anyone, it is because we are not able to touch the energy of loving kindness that exists everywhere in the cosmos. It's like having a radio to tune in to the radio station we like without having a battery.

If we see a small insect drowning and we are not moved to help it, we have no energy of loving kindness in us. But if we help the insect, suddenly we reach out to the cosmos. Loving kindness becomes real, and we feel joy. That joy is born because we saved an insect.

Suffering is all around us. If we are aware, we can do a lot to reduce suffering. We should not ignore or close our eyes when we see suffering; we should reach out to those who suffer. Touching suffering kindles the energy of compassion in us. Compassion brings joy and peace.

Anything we do or think or feel resonates throughout the cosmos. Therefore when you smile happily, you help the whole cosmos. When someone out there in the cosmos practices loving kindness, you benefit from his or her practice here.

When a mother takes care of her baby, she takes care of everyone around her and all the bodhisattvas in the cosmos. You don't have to do everything; you just do one thing well, and everything else is taken care of. If you do something good, joyful, happy, for your own benefit and the benefit of your family, that action will profit everyone in the cosmos. The Buddha was just one person, but his way of peace, joy, and happiness has penetrated the whole cosmos.

LEARNING TO LOVE

I often suggest to young people that they take two vows:

> 1) I vow to develop understanding in order to be able to live peacefully with people, animals, plants, and minerals.
>
> 2) I vow to develop compassion in order to protect the lives of people, animals, plants, and minerals.

In order to love, you need to understand, because love is made of understanding. If you do not understand someone, you cannot love him or her. Meditation is looking deeply to understand the needs and suffering of the other person. When you feel that you are understood, you feel love penetrating you. It's a wonderful feeling. All of us need understanding and love.

People like doing different things. Suppose your friend wants to play tennis after school, and you want to read a book. But because you want to make your friend happy, you put down your book and go out to play tennis with him. You are practicing understanding when you do this.

Through your understanding, you give your friend joy. When you make him happy, you become happy, too. This is an example of practicing understanding and loving.

Whenever you recite these two vows, ask yourself these questions: "Since I have made these vows, have I tried to learn about them? Have I tried to practice the vows?" I do not expect a yes or no answer to these questions. Even if you have tried to learn about the vows and have tried to practice them, it is not enough. The best way to respond to these questions is to open yourself and let the questions enter deeply into your whole being while you breathe in and out. Just by opening yourself to the questions and letting them enter, they will begin to work silently.

Understanding and love are the two most important teachings of the Buddha. If we do not make an effort to be open, to understand the suffering of other people, we will not be able to love them and to live in harmony with them. We should also try to understand and protect the lives of animals, plants, and minerals, and to live in harmony with them. If we cannot understand, we cannot love. The Buddha teaches us to look at living beings with the eyes of love and understanding. Please learn to practice this teaching.

RESPECTING SEX AND THE BODY

A person is made of body and mind. It is dangerous to communicate only with our bodies and not with our souls.

When we love each other, we want to be close to each other, but is it a closeness of souls with communication, understanding, and shared spiritual values? Then the coming together of two bodies has meaning and brings happiness. If two bodies come together without a coming together of souls, there will be suffering. Then we call the coming together of two bodies "empty sex."

Some parts of our bodies are very sacred, like the top of our head. The top of the head is an altar for Asian people, especially the Vietnamese, and we put the most sacred things on our altars. When we enter a house in Vietnam, even if it is very poor, there is always an ancestral altar with fruit, flowers, or incense. We treat the altar with great care, it is sacred. Similarly, there are sacred parts of our bodies that we don't want anyone to see or touch. This is true for girls and boys. We can hold someone's hand or put our hand on someone's shoulder, but we should not touch the sacred areas of the body. Our bodies are sacred like our souls, and we cannot share our bodies with just anybody.

There are also sacred areas in the soul that we don't want anyone to see or touch. There are experiences and images that we want to keep for ourselves. We don't want to share these with just anybody — only someone in whom we have the utmost confidence, the person we love the most. We reveal these confidences from the depths of our hearts to a very small number of people — probably only one person. Only when we have a friend who really understands us can we share these deeply sacred areas of our bodies and souls. Then the coming together of two bodies becomes the coming together of two souls, and it is a sacred ceremony that can bring about happiness.

When children of twelve, thirteen, or fourteen years have sex, what happens? Their two bodies come together, pushed along by sexual desire. The two children don't understand or know one another. And not knowing what love is, they have empty sex. It is dangerous, because these two young people might travel on the path of sexual desire where there is nothing but sex without understanding. In the future, they won't know what real love is. They are a fruit that is not yet ripe, a flower that has not yet opened.

The only way to become close to someone is through deep understanding, sharing each other's suffering and ideas. When we sleep with a person, we may feel that because we are close to him or her, we are communicating, but that is an illusion. In fact, the coming together of two bodies can bring about greater separation. Many people know that if they do not understand, love, or share deeply with their sexual partner, the lack of communication can lead to a huge rift between them. This is dangerous. We need to practice communication first by listening deeply and speaking lovingly.

Many of us look down on our bodies and souls, and we do not see their sacredness. If we are young, we have to protect our bodies and practice sexual responsibility. If we have sex without protecting the integrity of our body and our mind or the body and mind of the person we love, we are committing an offense against them and ourselves.

BE KIND TO YOURSELF

When you drink alcohol, smoke marijuana, or use drugs, you may at first feel good. But be aware that these feelings are very dangerous. They may lead to addiction and cause you much suffering. Please don't allow these seemingly pleasant feelings to fool you. You have to look mindfully into these feeling because they may contain the potential for painful feelings that will manifest in you later on.

That is why it is so important to be mindful of what you feel, drink, or eat. When we look into the liquor we are drinking, we can see many people who are at this very moment dying because of lack of food. Forty thousand children die every day because of lack of proper nutrition, and as you know, a lot of grain is used to make liquor. If you look deeply into that, you will no longer feel the pleasure of drinking; you will want to help prevent grain from being made into liquor so that people who are starving will have food to eat.

Consciousness is also a food. Believe it or not, when you read a magazine article, watch television, or go to the movies, you are ingesting consciousness, because these things reflect the collective consciousness of a group of people, with views, feelings, and so on. The Buddha said you have to be aware of the amount of consciousness you are ingesting. Some forms of consciousness are not good or healthy for you — especially if you are already in trouble.

For example, a television program, a book, or even the news we read in the newspaper can bring toxins into our consciousness if our fear, distress, and despair are nourished by such news, information, sights, and sounds. Advertising can also be toxic, and we should consider its messages carefully. Many companies promise that if we buy a certain product, we'll be happy: "Happiness is easy — just buy this." The sights and sounds that are used to capture our attention contain toxins that we have to protect ourselves against. If you continue to ingest this kind of consciousness, it will make you sick. That is why you need to mindfully select and ingest consciousnesses that will lead to your healing and transformation.

Mindful consumption means we bring into our body and mind only healthy food. We practice mindful eating, mindful drinking, not using alcohol or drugs, and not eating foods that contain toxins. We practice for ourselves and for the people in our family and society. The support of our family and friends can help us to do this.

ENJOYING ONE THING AT A TIME

Eating is sacred. Eating in mindfulness is a very deep and joyful practice that is easy to learn. It can increase the happiness of a family and a society.

Potato, English muffin, milk, we eat these foods every day but we don't know their nature, their origin, or the process involved in bringing them to our table. Before we eat, we can think about where the milk came from, the nature of milk, the situation of milk in the world. That can bring us insight, because very often when we drink milk, we don't know what it is — its origin, the happiness and suffering that is involved in milk.

It is a good idea to have a few minutes of collective meditation before we eat our meal. In the Christian tradition, someone at the table will say grace before the meal starts, but in the Buddhist tradition, we practice breathing mindfully before eating and looking deeply at the food on the table. We breathe in and out three times and thank the sunshine, the wheat field, the cloud that have brought us the wonderful food that we eat today.

Suppose you have an ice-cream cone. The ice cream is in the present moment — if it were in the past, you could not eat it. If it were in the future, how could you eat it? The ice cream exists only in the present moment. If your mind is in the past or the future, you are not really eating the ice cream. Come back to the here and now to eat the ice cream. Eat with all your being — body, heart, and mind. When you eat ice cream like that, you really know and enjoy the ice cream.

The secret of the practice is to do one thing at a time. If you eat ice cream, just eat ice cream, don't eat anything else. If you get excited, you eat your excitement, and the ice cream does not mean anything to you. If you get angry, then you eat your anger, and the food will not taste good. Eating ice cream is only eating ice cream.

Silence while eating helps us to appreciate the food and recognize its presence. During the first five minutes of eating, we can eat silently in order to focus our mind on our food. Try to eat silently for the first five minutes. Eat very slowly, enjoy the food you eat. Eat with all your being so that you deeply enjoy your food. You know that when you eat ice cream, if you eat slowly and mindfully, the ice cream will taste much better, and you will be happier. This is simple.

To be able to eat gives us great happiness. To have something to eat every day is a great happiness. You might consider saying, "Dad, I'm so happy. The casserole tonight is wonderful. Thank you." This kind of talking will bring about more happiness. If you blame someone at the table, if you criticize someone, saying, "How come you came home so late tonight?" it causes unhappiness for everyone. We have to live in such a way that dinnertime becomes the happiest time of the day.

If you can create happiness when you eat, you can create happiness in other moments of the day, and that's a wonderful thing to know about yourself. You have the gift of creating happiness at any moment.

Chasing Clouds

What is true happiness? Often we think that we cannot be happy if we don't get what we want. There are a million ways to be happy, but because we don't know how to open the door to happiness, we just chase after the things we want. The truth is, the more you chase after happiness, the more you suffer.

I have a nice story to tell you about a stream that descended from a mountaintop. The stream was very young, and her goal was to reach the ocean. She only wanted to run as quickly as possible. But when she got down to the plains, to the lowlands and the fields below, she slowed down; she became a river. A river cannot run as quickly as a young stream of water.

Flowing slowly along, she began to reflect the clouds in the sky. There were many kinds of clouds with many different forms and colors. Soon the river was spending all of her time chasing clouds, one after another. But the clouds would not stand still, they came and went, and she chased after them. When the river saw that no cloud wanted to stay with her, it made her very sad, and she cried.

One day, there was a strong wind that blew all the clouds away. The sky was magnificently blue. But because there were no clouds, the river began to think that life was not worth living anymore. She did not know how to enjoy the blue sky. She found the sky empty, and her life too seemed to have lost its meaning.

That night, her despair was so great that she wanted to kill herself. But how can a river kill herself? From someone you cannot become no one; from something, you cannot become nothing. All night long, the river cried, her tears lapping against the shore. That was the first time that she had gone back to herself. Before that, she had always run away from herself. Instead of looking for happiness inside, she had looked for it on the outside. So the first time she went back to herself and listened to the sound of her tears, she discovered something startling: she realized that she was, in fact, made of clouds.

It was strange. She had been chasing after clouds, thinking that she could not be happy without clouds, yet she herself was made of clouds. What she was seeking was already in her.

Happiness can be like that. If you know how to go back to the here and now, you will realize that the elements of your happiness are already available to you. You don't need to chase them anymore.

Suddenly, the river became aware of something reflecting on her cool, still surface. It was the blue sky. How peaceful, how solid, how free was that beautiful blue sky. This filled her with happiness. She was able to reflect the sky for the first time. Before that, she had only reflected the clouds and chased after them. She had completely ignored the presence of the intense, solid, blue sky that was always available to her. She had not noticed that her happiness was made of solidity, freedom, and space. That was a night of deep transformation, and her tears and suffering were transformed into joy and peace.

The next morning, the wind came up and the clouds returned. Now the river found that she could reflect the clouds with no attachment, with equanimity. Every time a cloud came, she said, "Hello, cloud." And when the cloud left, she was not sad at all and told it, "I will see you sometime later." She knew now that her freedom was the very foundation of her happiness. She had learned to stop and to not run anymore.

Then one night, something wonderful revealed itself to her: the image of a full moon reflected on her surface. It made her very happy. Holding hands with the clouds and the moon, she now made her way towards the ocean — but she was no longer in a hurry to reach it, she was enjoying every moment.

Each of us is a river.

Parallax Press publishes books and tapes on mindfulness practices and Buddhism. For a copy of our free catalog, please write to:

Parallax Press
P.O. Box 7355
Berkeley, California 94707
www.parallax.org

Thich Nhat Hanh has retreat communities in southwestern France (Plum Village), Vermont (Green Mountain Dharma Center), and California (Deer Park Monastery), where monks, nuns, laymen, and laywomen practice the art of mindful living.

Families and children are especially welcome at the Plum Village Summer Opening. For information, please visit www.plumvillage.org or write to:

Plum Village
13 Martineau
33580 Dieulivol
France

Green Mountain Dharma Center
P.O. Box 182
Hartland Four Corners, VT 05049

Deer Park Monastery
2499 Melru Lane
Escondido, CA 92026